Click, Clack, Boo!

For Rose M.
—D. C.

For Gaby
—B. L.

ATHENEUM BOOKS FOR YOUNG READERS
An imprint of Simon & Schuster Children's Publishing Division
1230 Avenue of the Americas, New York, New York 10020
Text copyright © 2013 by Doreen Cronin
Illustrations copyright © 2013 by Betsy Lewin
ATHENEUM BOOKS FOR YOUNG READERS is a registered trademark of
Simon & Schuster, Inc.
Atheneum logo is a trademark of Simon & Schuster, Inc.
For information about special discounts for bulk purchases, please contact Simon &
Schuster Special Sales at 1-866-506-1949 or business@simonandschuster.com.
The Simon & Schuster Speakers Bureau can bring authors to your live event.
For more information or to book an event, contact the Simon & Schuster Speakers
Bureau at 1-866-248-3049 or visit our website at www.simonspeakers.com.
Book design by Ann Bobco
The text for this book is set in Filosofia.
The illustrations for this book are rendered in brush and watercolor.
Manufactured in China
0513 SCP

First Edition
10 9 8 7 6 5 4 3 2 1
Library of Congress Cataloging-in-Publication Data
Cronin, Doreen.
Click, clack, boo!: a tricky treat / Doreen Cronin ; illustrated by Betsy Lewin. — 1st ed.
p. cm.
Summary: Farmer Brown does not like Halloween, but the animals hold a Halloween
party in his barn.
ISBN 978-1-4424-6553-4
ISBN 978-1-4424-6554-1 (eBook)
[1. Halloween—Fiction. 2. Domestic animals—Fiction. 3. Animals—Fiction.]
I. Lewin, Betsy, ill. II. Title.
PZ7.C88135Cb 2014
[E]—dc23   2012014537

Click, Clack, Boo!
A tricky treat

Doreen Cronin *and* **Betsy Lewin**

Atheneum

Atheneum Books for Young Readers

New York London Toronto

Farmer Brown does not like Halloween.

Witches give him nightmares.

Pirates give him shivers.

Jack-o'-lanterns flicker spooky shadows
on the wall.

Farmer Brown leaves a bowl of candy
on the porch.

He puts up a DO NOT DISTURB sign.
He draws the shades and locks the door.

But in the barn
the Halloween party
has just begun.

There is a
crunch,
      crunch,
            crunching
as the mice scurry across the field.

There is a

creak,
creak,
creaking

as the sheep slowly push open
the barn door.

There is a

tap,
tap,
tapping,

and the cows go to the window
to let the cats in.

Farmer Brown does not like the sounds
of Halloween night.
He checks the lock on the door.

He peeks through
the window.

There is a dark creature
standing beneath
the trees.

Farmer Brown runs to his room,
pulls on his pajamas,
and climbs under the covers.

He hears the

crunch,

crunch,

crunching

of leafy footsteps
heading toward the house.

There is a
creak,

creak,

creaking

on the old boards
of the front porch.

Then a
tap,

tap,

tapping

on the front door.

Farmer Brown pulls up his covers tight.

He hears a

quack,

quack,

quackle

in the crisp night air.

Farmer Brown jumps out of bed.

The porch is empty.
The candy bowl is gone.

There is a new note on
Farmer Brown's door:

Farmer Brown runs to the barn.

There is a **creak,
creak,
creaking**
on the old boards of the front porch . . .

and a **crunch,
crunch,
crunching**
of leafy footsteps heading
toward the barn.

There is a **tap, tap, tapping** on the window.

BEST
COSTUME